This book belongs to

_____

MICKEY'S WEATHER MACHINE

Disney's

READ and GROW LIBRARY

Published by Advance Publishers
Winter Park, Florida

Written by Sharon Shavers Gayle   Edited by Bonnie Brook
Penciled by Len Smith   Painted by Cindi Bothner
Designed by Design Five
Cover art by Peter Emslie
Cover design by Irene Yap

ISBN: 1-885222-88-2
10 9 8 7 6 5 4 3 2 1

One evening, while Morty and Ferdie were getting ready for bed, a big snowstorm began.

"Oh, no!" Ferdie cried. "We were supposed to collect rocks tomorrow for show-and-tell. Now the snowstorm has ruined everything!"

"Why does it snow in the winter, Uncle Mickey?" asked Morty.

Mickey thought for a moment. "Gosh, I sure wish the Windi Weather machine were here to answer your questions."

"The Windi Weather machine? What's that?" asked Ferdie.

"Well, back when I was your age, I was given a wonderful birthday present," said Mickey. "It could answer any question about the weather."

"Any question?" Morty asked in a very sleepy voice.

"That's right," answered Mickey. "And, best of all, it could take you anywhere you wanted to go to find out about the weather firsthand. All you had to do was—well, gosh, boys, just look outside." Mickey pointed out the window.

5

When the boys looked outside, they saw an old-fashioned airplane sitting in the snow.

"Wow!" exclaimed Ferdie. "Is that the Windi Weather machine, Uncle Mickey?"

"It sure is!" Mickey answered. Suddenly, he had a bright idea. "Boys, let's learn about the weather!"

"*Blip! Blip! Blip!* It's time for an adventure," Windi's radio announced. "Just climb aboard, and I'll guide you through the seasons."

"Well, boys, what are we waiting for?" said Mickey. "Let's take Windi Weather for a spin." As soon as they climbed aboard, Windi took off.

Soon Mickey, Morty, and Ferdie found themselves in the middle of a winter wonderland.

"Let's go ice-skating!" Morty exclaimed.

"Look," said Mickey. "Windi even brought you ice skates."

After the boys had skated around the lake, Ferdie asked, "Why does the lake freeze in the winter?"

"It's colder in the winter," came the voice from Windi's radio. "When the water cools off, it eventually freezes or becomes solid. The cold also freezes rain and makes it into snow."

"Boy, Uncle Mickey, Windi sure knows a lot of stuff about winter," said Morty, very impressed.

"Look! Windi brought us a sled, too!" said Ferdie. Seconds later, Mickey, Morty, and Ferdie were sledding down a snowy slope.

At the bottom of the hill, the sled came to rest in front of a cave. Inside, a bear was snoring peacefully.

"I'm glad we didn't wake him," Ferdie whispered.

"That bear's in a very deep sleep called hibernation," Mickey explained. "In the winter, some animals, like bears and squirrels, fall asleep and live off the food they have eaten during the warmer months."

"Hey," said Morty, looking around. "It's still early, but the sun is beginning to set."

"That's because during the winter, the earth tilts away from the sun. We get less sunlight every day. That makes it feel colder, and the daylight doesn't last as long," Windi's radio reported.

"Well," said Mickey, "since our day is almost over, I think it's time to go!"

They climbed back aboard Windi and soon found themselves flying to a brand-new season.

"Where are we?" Morty and Ferdie asked.

"It's spring," said Mickey, "and we're on a farm."

"Look at all the baby animals!" cried Morty.

"Not only is spring a time for new flowers and plants to bloom," crackled Windi's radio, "but it's also the time of year when horses, cows, sheep, and pigs are born."

"Let's see what else Windi can show us about spring," said Mickey, as they climbed back aboard Windi.

A little while later, Morty and Ferdie hopped out of Windi and looked around.

"Wow, it sure is *windy*," Morty giggled.

"You know," said Mickey, "I seem to remember that Windi has some kites in the storage compartment."

Soon the boys were flying their kites up, up, and away.

"Yippee!" said Ferdie. "Why is it so windy?"

"The air is getting warmer," Windi's radio replied. "Warm air sometimes fights with the leftover cold air of winter. That's what causes great gusts of wind to happen during the spring."

"Spring is also the season when all the birds and animals that went south for the winter come home," said Mickey as the boys scrambled up a ladder to peer at a bird's nest. "It's the time for the animals who have gone to sleep to wake up and begin looking for food."

Just then, big, fat raindrops began to fall.

Mickey pulled some rain gear out of Windi's storage compartment.

"Hey! This is fun," said Ferdie, playing in the rain. "It sure does rain a lot in the springtime."

"Rain helps the plants grow new leaves and flowers," Windi's radio said.

"Ah-ah-ah-choo!" sneezed Mickey suddenly.

"Blip! Blip! Blip!" Windi's radio announced. "Time to get to warmer weather!"

Soon Mickey, Morty, and Ferdie were in swimming
trunks, playing by a beautiful, big, blue lake.

"That warm summer air sure feels good," said Morty.

"Not only is the weather warmer," said Ferdie, jumping into the lake with a splash, "but the days are longer, too. We can stay out here forever!"

"That's because during the summer the earth tilts back toward the sun," Windi's radio announced. "We get more sunlight every day. That makes it feel warmer, and daylight lasts longer."

"That's the opposite of winter!" cried Morty.

"Almost," Mickey replied.

"Summer is my favorite season," said Ferdie.

"Ah," said Mickey, "that's because it's when most families take vacations."

"May we take a vacation, Uncle Mickey?" Morty asked.

Windi flashed her lights. Then her radio clicked on. "I know the perfect place."

Mickey, Morty, and Ferdie jumped back in the plane.

Soon Windi landed in the middle of a cornfield.

"The corn's so high!" shouted Morty and Ferdie as they jumped out.

"Farmers take extra-special care of their crops during the summer to make sure that there is plenty of food to eat during the winter," said Windi's radio.

"Speaking of food," said Mickey, "let's eat!" He pulled a picnic basket filled with goodies from Windi's cockpit.

Soon night fell, and the darkened sky was filled with summer fireworks. Mickey, Morty, and Ferdie watched the sky while they ate.

"Those fireworks are great," said Ferdie.

"So is this picnic," said Morty. "I love the lemonade the best. I could drink it all day long."

"I like apple cider," said Ferdie, "but we have to wait until fall for that."

"Blip! Blip! Blip!" sounded Windi's radio.

"Climb in, boys," Mickey said from Windi's cockpit. "It sounds as if Windi's ready to take us into our next season."

This time Windi landed right in Mickey's backyard.

"Wow," said Morty. "It's windy like spring."

"What season is this?" asked Ferdie.

"It's fall," answered Mickey.

"This time the air is getting colder," explained Windi's radio. "It's fighting with the leftover warm air from summer to cause these gusts of wind."

"Why do leaves turn different colors during the fall?" Morty asked Windi.

"During the summer, trees make special chemicals that keep their leaves green," Windi's radio explained. "But they can't do that in the cold, so the green fades. Then the leaves change color and fall off."

"Trees collect food through their leaves during the summer," said Mickey. "They save enough food so that they can shed their leaves during the colder months."

"And sleep during the winter like that bear we saw," Ferdie giggled.

"I guess you could say that," said Mickey, smiling.

"Another important thing that happens during fall is that the crops which have grown throughout the summer are finally ready to be picked. This is called harvest time," said Windi's radio.

"These apples sure look ready to be picked," Morty said, as he plucked one off a tree.

"Here's your apple cider, Ferdie," said Mickey, handing his nephew a glass.

Suddenly, Mickey, Morty, and Ferdie heard the familar *"Blip! Blip! Blip!"* from Windi's radio. "Time for me to rest," the radio announced.

"That's right," said Mickey. "It's time for *all* of us to rest."

"Aw, Uncle Mickey . . ." Morty protested. But as soon as he and Ferdie reached their beds, they fell fast asleep.

The next morning, Morty and Ferdie woke up to see snow covering Uncle Mickey's backyard.

"Boy, I had some dream!" exclaimed Ferdie. "I dreamed we went flying around in that weather machine Uncle Mickey told us about last night."

"I had the same dream!" shouted Morty. "Let's go find Uncle Mickey and tell him all about it."

When the boys got to the garage, a big surprise
was waiting for them. There was Mickey working on
an airplane that looked curiously like the Windi
Weather machine.

"Maybe it wasn't a dream after all," Morty said.

"Maybe not!" Ferdie answered.

And maybe—just maybe—they were about to have
the best show-and-tell their school had ever seen!